Angelina Ballerina™
Sleepover Party!

Based on the stories by Katharine Holabird
Based on the illustrations by Helen Craig

Ready-to-Read

Simon Spotlight
New York   London   Toronto   Sydney   New Delhi

SIMON SPOTLIGHT

An imprint of Simon & Schuster Children's Publishing Division

1230 Avenue of the Americas, New York, New York 10020

This Simon Spotlight edition August 2020

Illustrations by Andrew Grey

© 2020 Helen Craig Ltd. and Katharine Holabird.

The Angelina Ballerina name and character and the dancing Angelina logo are trademarks of HIT Entertainment Limited, Katharine Holabird, and Helen Craig.

SIMON SPOTLIGHT, READY-TO-READ, and colophon are registered trademarks of Simon & Schuster, Inc.

For information about special discounts for bulk purchases, please contact Simon & Schuster Special Sales at 1-866-506-1949 or business@simonandschuster.com.

Manufactured in the United States of America 0720 LAK

10 9 8 7 6 5 4 3 2 1

ISBN 978-1-5344-6954-9 (hc)

ISBN 978-1-5344-6953-2 (pbk)

ISBN 978-1-5344-6955-6 (eBook)

It was a beautiful evening
in Chipping Cheddar.
Angelina Ballerina
was having
her very first sleepover!

Flora and Felicity arrived
with their bags.

"Welcome!" Angelina said.

The three girls dressed up
in fancy costumes.

"We should do
a special sleepover dance,"
Felicity said.

Angelina and Flora thought that was a great idea!

They jumped,
leaped, and twirled.

At the end
they pretended
to fall asleep.

"That was lovely!"
Mrs. Mouseling said.

"Now, come inside.
It is dinner time."

They ate pizza, salad,
and cheddarburgers.

Everything tasted
yummy!

After dinner
the girls laid out
their sleeping bags.

They changed into
their pajamas.

Then they read a book
called *Sleeping Mouse*.

"I love fairy tales," Flora said.

Soon Mrs. Mouseling
turned off the lights.

Angelina and her friends
continued talking
in the dark.

"When I grow up
I want to be a
real ballerina!"
Angelina whispered.

"You will be the best
ballerina ever,"
Flora whispered back.

Felicity fell asleep
right away,
but Flora did not.

She felt nervous about
sleeping in a new place.

"I will hold your hand,"
Angelina said.

"Thank you," Flora said.
Soon they were all asleep.

The next morning
Angelina and her friends
ate pancakes
for breakfast.

Soon it was time
for Flora and Felicity
to go home.

"When can we have another sleepover?" they asked.

"Soon!" Angelina said.
"Sleepovers are the best!"